Pokémon

Save Those Mudkip!

**Adapted by
Tracey West and
Katherine Noll**

OFFICIAL Pokémon EXPERT'S CLUB

SCHOLASTIC INC.

New York Toronto London Auckland Sydney
Mexico City New Delhi Hong Kong Buenos Aires

Published by Scholastic Inc.
90 Old Sherman Turnpike, Danbury, CT 06816.

SCHOLASTIC and associated logos are trademarks and/or registered trademarks of
Scholastic Inc.

ISBN-10: 0-439-72179-2
ISBN-13: 978-0-439-72179-0

First Scholastic Printing, February 2005

One day, Ash and his friends were heading to a new Pokémon Gym.

"I bet if we keep following this river, we will find some new Pokémon," Max said.

But their path was blocked by a giant waterfall.

Ash looked up. "What do we do now?" he asked.

"Not even a Magikarp could climb *that* waterfall," said Max.

"I have an idea," Brock said. "Lotad, go!"

Lotad, a Water Pokémon, popped out of its Poké Ball.

Brock tied a rock to a long rope. He threw it in the air.

Lotad used Water Gun. The water blast sent the rope around a tree at the top of the falls. Then they all climbed up the rope.

The group walked along
the muddy riverbank.
"Look!" Max said.
"Those look like Mudkip!"
"Those are *baby*
Mudkip!" Brock
added.

"They are cute," May said. "I want to catch one!"

May ran toward the baby Mudkip. But a big Mudkip jumped in front of her. It blasted May with Water Gun!

Everyone laughed.
Just then one of the baby
Mudkip fell into the river!

"Lotad, go help!" Brock yelled.

Lotad swam out to the baby Mudkip. It put the baby on its flat head.

But the river was too strong. So the big Mudkip jumped into the water. It saved Lotad and the baby Mudkip!

"Thanks," Brock said.

But the big Mudkip was shy. It ran away. Just then a strange-looking man popped out of the bushes.

"It is a Mudkip monster!" Ash yelled.

"I am not a monster," the man said. "My name is Swampy. And you had better not steal my baby Mudkip!"

"We were just trying to help," Max said. "This baby Mudkip fell into the river."

"In that case, come to my house for tea," Swampy said.

They went to his house. Swampy talked and talked.

"I should not tell you this," said Swampy. "But I raise Mudkip for the Pokémon League. My Mudkip go to new Trainers."

Swampy showed them some blue eggs.

"These are Mudkip eggs," he said. "Look, one is about to hatch!"

Ash and his friends watched the baby Mudkip hatch.

"We saw a big Mudkip this morning," Brock said. "Do you know it?"

"That is a wild one," Swampy said. "It protects my baby Mudkip. But I worry that it is getting too big for a Trainer."

Nearby, Team Rocket was trying to find Ash and his friends.

"Where did those little twerps go?" Jessie asked.

"Maybe they are behind this fence," Meowth said.

"But how will we get through it?" asked James.

"Go, Seviper!"
Jessie yelled.

Her Poison Pokémon blasted out of its Poké Ball. But Seviper could not break the fence.

Then James tried. "Come on, Cacnea!" he cried.

Cacnea, a Grass Pokémon, came out of its Poké Ball. But it did not attack the fence. It slammed into James!

James flew into the fence. "Ow!" he cried. The fence broke! Team Rocket stepped through.

Ash and his friends heard the noise. They ran to the fence.

But Brock saw the wild Mudkip. He ran after it, instead.

"Let me be your friend," Brock said. "Try some of my Pokémon food."

But the wild Mudkip did not trust Brock. It would not eat.

At the fence, Team Rocket jumped out.

"I hope those bad guys do not try to steal my baby Mudkip," Swampy said. "If the dam breaks, the baby Mudkip would have nowhere to live."

"What a great idea!" said Meowth.

"I should not have said that!" Swampy moaned.

"Cacnea, use Needle Arm to break that dam!" James yelled.

Cacnea slammed into James again. James flew into the dam. The dam broke!

Down the river, Brock saw the dam break. A big wave of water rushed toward all of the baby Mudkip.

Brock threw out a Poké Ball. "Forretress, go!" he yelled. "Use Rapid Spin!"

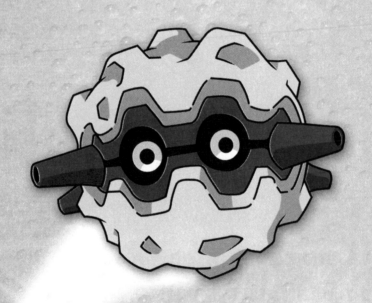

Forretress began to spin around and around. It held back the wave of water.

Brock, Lotad, and the wild Mudkip jumped into the river. They rescued the babies.

"Oh no!" Brock yelled. "There is still one left!"

The wild Mudkip dove into the water. It grabbed the last baby. But they could not swim back to shore. The water carried them over the falls! The wild Mudkip grabbed a rock. But it could not hold on for long.

Brock grabbed the rope he had used to climb up the falls. He tied it around himself and jumped!

"Mudkip! Grab my hand!" he said.

But the wild Mudkip was afraid. "Please," Brock said. "You have to trust me."

Finally, the wild Mudkip reached out for Brock. Brock held on while Ash and his friends pulled up the rope. Everyone was safe.

Before anyone could rest, there was a loud noise.

Team Rocket stomped up.
They were in a robot that looked
like a giant girl!

"Let's grab some Mudkip!"
Meowth yelled.
    The robot scooped
up all of the babies.
It dropped them into
a big sack.

Brock knew what to do.

"Lotad, Mudkip, use your Water Gun attack!" he yelled. "Soak the ground with water!"

The two Pokémon blasted water onto the ground at the robot's feet.

The ground turned to mud. The robot sank into the soft mud.

Then the wild Mudkip jumped up. It grabbed the sack with the baby Mudkip. It set them free!

"Go, Pikachu!" Ash yelled. "Give them a Thunderbolt!"

Pikachu shocked the robot. The attack sent Team Rocket blasting off into the sky.

"I am so proud of you, Mudkip,"
Brock said.

"Can you take this Mudkip with
you?" Swampy asked. "I know you
will take good care of it, Brock."

Brock smiled at Mudkip. "How
do you feel about that?"

Mudkip smiled back at Brock. *"Mudkip! Mudkip!"* it cried.

They hugged. "Yay!" Brock cheered. "From now on, it is you and me, Mudkip."

Max said, "I knew we would find new Pokémon on this trip!"

Who's That
Water
Pokémon?

See page 45 for the answer!

Fishy Tails

Can you tell who these Water Pokémon are by just looking at their tails?

3.

4.

7.

8.

39

Check page 45 or your *Water Pokédex* for the answers.

Battle Time!

Now it is your turn to battle! Read about each battle below. Then pick the best Pokémon to use against your opponent. In each battle, all of the Pokémon are the same level.

1. *Splash!* Milotic pops out of your opponent's Poké Ball. Which Pokémon will you choose to beat this beautiful Water Type?

Blaziken™
(Fire/Fighting)

Sceptile™
(Grass)

Regirock™
(Rock)

2. Trapinch, a Ground Pokémon, is ready to battle next. Which of these Pokémon is most likely to take it down?

Remoraid™
(Water)

Ampharos™
(Electric)

Arcanine™
(Fire)

3. Look out! Here comes Cacnea, a creepy Grass Pokémon. If you want to beat it, which Pokémon should you choose?

Donphan™
(Ground)

Ariados™
(Bug/Poison)

Huntail™
(Water)

Check page 45 or your
Pokédex books for
the answers.

Know Your Names!

In each row, two of the Water Pokémon have names that begin with the same letter. One of the Pokémon does not. Can you pick out the Pokémon that doesn't belong with the other two?

4.

5.

6.

7.

Check page 45 or your *Water Pokédex* for the answers!

Water Pokémon Jokes

What does one Squirtle use to call another Squirtle?

A shell-phone!

Why is a Feebas easy to weigh?

Because it has its own scales!

What did Misty say to Psyduck?

You quack me up!

Why does Krabby never share?

Because it's shell-fish!

What does a Politoed write on?

A lily pad!

What do you get when you cross a Phanpy with a Remoraid?

Swimming trunks!

Answers

Page 37: Who's That Water Pokémon?

Corphish!

Pages 38–39: Fishy Tails

1. Carvanha
2. Seaking
3. Totodile
4. Squirtle
5. Gorebyss
6. Mudkip
7. Gyarados
8. Slowbro

Pages 40–41: Battle Time!

1. Sceptile (Grass beats Water)
2. Remoraid (Water beats Ground)
3. Ariados (Bug/Poison beats Grass)

Pages 42–43: Know Your Names!

1. Totodile. Mudkip and Marill begin with *M*.
2. Goldeen. Clamperl and Corsola begin with *C*.
3. Feraligatr. Krabby and Kyogre begin with *K*.
4. Wingull. Squirtle and Spheal begin with *S*.
5. Starmie. Wooper and Wailmer begin with *W*.
6. Lanturn. Barboach and Blastoise begin with *B*.
7. Sharpedo. Poliwag and Politoed begin with *P*.